A MAN AND A DOG

DUANE HEWITT

A MAN AND A DOG

Hushion House
PUBLISHING

A MAN AND A DOG

National Library of Canada Cataloguing in Publication

Hewitt, Duane, 1958 –
A man and a dog / Duane Hewitt.

ISBN 0-9733212-2-9

I. Title.
PS8565.E899M35 2004   C813'.54   C2003-907216-9

Hushion House Publishing Limited
www.hushion.com

To contact the author or the publisher, please write:
P.O. Box 455
31 Adelaide Street East
Toronto, Ontario
M5C 2J5
Toll free: 1-888-272-2152

Special thanks to Matthew Ledger for jacket and title design
Contact: www.atomicgardenmedia.com
Book interior design by Patrick O'Malley
Author photo: Ken Mulveney, Toronto

Printed and bound in Canada

For the homeless,
and
for those who believe in them.

The man slept in the streets of the downtown. He took what handouts he could during the day, foraging and begging on those evenings when he did not go to the hostel. He was not aged, decrepit or disturbed, but he was alone. The years had thrown much his way (in the manner that life does), yet he showed only a hint of the joys and miseries he had endured. If one were to look closely, they would see a face that was fond of laughing, for there were lines near his eyes that develop for those who are able to find humour in all that assails them. Yet there was also a sagging under the eyes and puffiness to the cheeks that revealed a man who had cried much in his time. He was lean, indeed thin, for he ate infrequently as only fate and circumstance allowed. His skin was weathered; tanned and toughened by years of sun, rain, wind, dust and smog.

He was not an unhappy man for, though he knew his situation well, he was able to find bits of joy. He still had most of his teeth (though they, too, were spoiled), and he liked to look into the sky and smile as if seeing something others could not see, or awaiting the appearance of some otherworldly presence.

"Let me look," he would mutter to himself, and then he would trail off, holding his hand to his eyes to block the sun as he smiled. Then he would continue on his way.

His face was familiar to many, and most who knew him thought him to be harmless though they might have viewed him as eccentric. He had come to be known in areas that he frequented and though he kept mostly to himself, he was friendly and could at times be outgoing. People who knew and helped him called him Alfred, Fred or Freddie, but he was also known as Jim, Jimmy and John. He was grateful when someone gave him money, food, or anything useful and was careful to say, "thank you," but others had also heard him swear or curse at them from behind and so there were those who chose to keep away from him.

He did not think much about the future, and was for the most part content living day by day. Some had tried to help him get "on his feet," but he never felt he was off his feet and didn't understand why there was such a fuss worrying about tomorrow when it was always today. There had been tough times for him in the past but everything always seemed to turn out or be, as he said, "just as it was."

He slept on the streets for the most part, especially during the warmer months when he carried an old roll with him. It was a dirty and torn sleeping bag that was very thin but it suited him well. He tended to leave it at some of his favourite spots during the day when he didn't want to carry it and once it had been stolen. It troubled him that day but he was lucky because it was such a warm week in July that he didn't need it anyway. He eventually found it on another side street, different from where he left it, but he didn't give it any thought. He was happy to have it back.

When it grew cold, or when the weather was particularly bad, he sometimes slept under an overpass. It was a big area with dirt and grass and trees and it kept the elements away. The first time he tried sleeping there the sounds of the traffic overhead bothered him, but then it began to sound comforting – like the sound of a heartbeat, and so he slept well. A few others of similar means knew about this secret refuge and shared it on occasion, but they left each other alone and so it was good.

Sometimes he would go to one of the men's hostels where they knew him and would give him clothes and food, but he always found it crowded and it seemed to infringe on his sense of privacy. Once, he woke up in the middle of the night and said, "This is not good," and so he left, choosing instead to go to one of the derelict buildings he knew where he would climb through a broken window and find a better place to sleep.

He developed a terrible cough once. It hit him in late February when the winter was especially harsh and he had eaten sparingly. He would wake up in the middle of the night coughing so hard that he was sure he had pneumonia or something equally bad. A young volunteer at the hostel saw how bad he was and managed to get her hands on some penicillin. She tried to get him to stay and get better but he wanted to leave. She made him promise he would tell her where he was sleeping and so she visited him at the old vacant Berrings factory where she continued to see him, bringing him food, blankets and more penicillin. By the arrival of late April and warmer weather, he had recovered and was grateful to her but he made no effort to stay in touch with her.

When he met the dog he was lying on the corner of Bourbon Street, drifting in and out of sleep. The dog approached from down the block and when he saw the man, he stopped to look. He was a good-size dog, about 50 pounds, with white and tan markings and a broad, heavy back. He might have been a cross between an English bulldog with pit bull or terrier, because he had a long narrow snout with eyes that were almost pink. The dog was muscular (mostly in the forequarters), and there were scars on his back though they had healed from long ago. This was a dog that clearly could have been capable of much (in the way that dogs are), but he had a good disposition and there was nothing more about him than to say he simply wanted to go his own way and be left alone.

When the dog appeared, the man seemed harmless to the dog and so the dog stood watching and then decided the man was safe to approach. The man was muttering to himself but the dog, making no sense of it, decided to ignore the man's rambling and went forward to sniff. There was the stale smell of alcohol, soiled clothing and other old odours, but nothing the dog found distasteful or untrustworthy. He lowered his head gently, keeping his eyes forward on the man, and went to lay next to him.

It was mid-afternoon by the time the man roused from his sleep and saw the dog there next to him. The man shook his head and ran his fingers through his silver-grey hair. As the dog began to stir, the man said, "What have we here?"

The dog raised his head and, standing, said, "The warmth of two is always better than that of one."

The man looked at the dog and nodded, deciding this was true, and replied, "Yes, that is so – but this is August and it is not cold."

"Well," said the dog, "it is not always just the time of year or type of day that determines whether one is cold or not."

The man thought about this and decided, yes, that was true also. So they both acknowledged that they were in agreement and got up to walk.

Their stroll carried them down a series of short

streets where shops and cafés opened onto the sidewalk. They passed the odd fruit stand, bakery, delicatessen and at one point, when they neared a butcher shop, the owner was there at the door. The butcher was rotund though not short, and he wore a long white apron. He saw the man and greeted him by holding up his hand. Then he saw the dog. "Ah," said the butcher, "I have not seen you this week. You have a friend I see."

The man said yes, though he did not know the name of his new friend, and the butcher said, "That does not matter. I have something for the both of you."

The butcher asked the man to wait as he went inside. When he came back, he passed the man a long roll of French bread and a package of brown wrapping, "with salami and turkey," he said. Then he pulled out a big, heavily wrapped package and said, "Take this for him," as he motioned to the dog. "It is a good beef shank bone with meat and he will like it."

The dog looked up at the butcher and then at the man. The dog licked his chops but said nothing.

"He will love it," spoke the man. "I will carry it for him. We are grateful."

The man and the butcher waved good-bye to each other as the man and the dog continued on their way. The man was clearly pleased.

"That was very good of him," said the dog. "He must care for you that he would be so generous."

"He is a kind man," said the man, "and now you have me to carry your bone for you, or would you like to have it now?"

"I have nowhere to put it," said the dog. "Had I been alone I would have had to carry it a long ways until I could find a place to hide it."

"Ah," said the man thinking about this. "But then that means that, like me, you have no place to stay and now you have me to help you."

"Yes," said the dog, "now I have you to help me and that is good."

The man smiled again and as they walked, the dog seemed to trot with a happier gait.

They said nothing between them as they continued onward. The dog thought that the man would surely be hungry and wondered why he hadn't stopped to eat the French loaf with the meat, but knew the man had his own will.

They walked for a ways and then came to a variety store on the corner of Desmond and Donald streets. People came and went from the store and it was obvious that the store sold a bit of everything, including beer and wine.

"We will stop here," said the man, "and see if someone will give us some money so that we can buy a small bottle of wine for our supper."

They waited near the front of the store (though not at the door, but to the side) and the man brought out a little tin cup that had been painted white with some roughly sketched flowers and a big "$" that had been drawn in heavy black ink. It was now late in the afternoon and the man knew that people would soon be on their way back from work and there would be more customers stopping at the store. As they stood with the tin cup, the man explained this and the dog agreed it was a good plan.

"And then you will have a happy little feast," said the dog, "and I will have my bone."

Together they stood there for several hours. Some people gave little bits of change whereas others gave nothing. Sometimes someone would approach and smile at the dog and then pat him, which he did not mind. Once they had collected a few coins, the man would shake the tin to attract attention. Eventually a well-dressed man approached and remarked that the dog was a fine animal indeed.

"A handsome animal," said the stranger. "It would be a sad thing if he did not eat." And then the stranger gave the man a $20 bill and said that hunger was an especially hard thing for those who did not understand it.

The man took the money and smiled, bending over in a bow and thanking the stranger. After the stranger went into the store and then came out to continue on his way, he told the man and the dog that he wished them well. Then he was gone.

The dog looked up at the man and the man was

again pleased. He said that now he could get his bottle of wine and that he would be out shortly, apologizing that the store would not allow a dog to enter.

"That is okay," said the dog. "It is not my place to be and I haven't the pockets or the means to buy anything anyway."

The man nodded and went into the store. When he came back out, he had a large paper bag with him and he put the loaf of bread and the other two packages the butcher had given them into the bag to make it easier to carry. Then he said they should go now.

After they had walked for a while, the dog said, "It was very good of that stranger to help us so."

"Yes," said the man, "it was good."

They walked a bit further and then the dog said, "He knew hunger, that man. He did not look it but he knew its hardship and had tasted hunger himself."

The man looked at the dog and thought about this. He did not say anything but he frowned a little. Then he said, "Why do you think that?"

"Well," said the dog, "no one man possesses hunger, yet all are affected by it. That stranger understood this."

"Oh," said the man. But the man said nothing more and the dog could tell he was in thought.

They wove their way through the streets to one of the abandoned old buildings where the man sometimes stayed. They approached a boarded-up door and the man pried away two wooden planks. Then he stood aside to allow the dog to enter.

"After you," he said to the dog as he held the door open.

The dog thanked him and they both went in. The building was old and unused, but it was spacious and air circulated freely within. The man led the dog to a corner of a big room where there was a big desk and on that desk were candles. The man opened a drawer and pulled out some matches and then lit the candles. When the dog saw this he was very pleased.

"Ah," said the dog, "light!"

The man would not have noticed but if a dog could smile then there would have been a smile to be seen on the face of the dog.

The man went around the desk and pulled two old blankets from a big cardboard box. He spread them on the floor before the desk and invited the dog to make himself comfortable. The blankets were torn and dirty but the dog did not mind. The dog sat on the corner of one of the blankets and watched as the man sat down and pulled the food and wine from the bag.

"And now," said the man, "we will eat."

He put the loaf of bread on the desk and then opened the package the butcher had given them containing the turkey and salami. He took two strips of meat from the package and passed them to the dog, who accepted them readily. But the dog did not eat. He sat the meat before him and waited.

"You do not eat," said the man. "Are you not hungry?"

"I wait for you," said the dog, "that we may dine together."

The man looked at him quizzically and then picked up the loaf of bread. He tore it down the middle as best he could and put some meat into the loaf. Then he opened the bottle of wine and took a drink.

"If you were not a dog," said the man, "I would offer you some wine. It is very good."

"That is okay," said the dog, "I do not need the wine – it is yours to enjoy. But it would be good if I had some water later."

"Ah, yes," said the man, "there is water here and I will get it for the both of us when we are done."

The dog watched the man take another drink but said nothing. Then the man picked up the loaf with meat and began to eat. Still, the dog waited and did nothing.

"Again you do not eat?" said the man. "What is the matter?"

"There is no matter," said the dog.

"Well then, why is it that you wait?" asked the man.

"I do not wait," answered the dog. "I was giving thanks."

The man stopped eating and looked at the

dog. "Thanks?" said the man. "What do you know of 'thanks'?"

The dog was quiet for a moment more and then spoke. "That is the point," said the dog, "I would not presume to know. But here we have food, wine and shelter when earlier today we were both cold, hungry and alone. Now we are well. And together tonight we shall be warm."

The man seemed to be thinking about this but said little more. Then they both began to eat in silence with the man sharing his meat with the dog.

They ate for a while and it was good. When they finished the salami and turkey the man reached into the big brown paper bag and pulled out a small box. The box contained some special biscuits that he bought for the dog.

"Here," said the man, "these are for you."

The man opened the box and passed the dog some biscuits. They were fresh and good and the dog was very pleased.

"Ah," said the dog, "you honour me. This is truly a pleasant surprise and now I humbly give thanks to you, good friend."

The man paused as he thought about this and he gave the dog another biscuit. The dog accepted the biscuit graciously and so the man and the dog were both happy. When the dog finished the biscuits, which he found to be very delicious, he said, "This has all been quite wonderful. A very blessed thing."

They both lay down together in the blankets and made themselves comfortable. The man gave the dog his bone and the man continued to drink his wine. Together they were silent, enjoying the food in their stomachs and the quiet friendship between them.

Eventually the man rose and said, "You have not had water. I should get it for you before we both fall asleep so as to quench your thirst."

The man went to another room far off in the building where he knew of a faucet that leaked water. When he returned, he carried a bowl of water for the dog and a glass of water for himself. He set the bowl of water down beside the dog and the dog was pleased.

"Now," said the dog, "we can drink and we can rest."

It was getting dark outside and the light of the candles cast long flickering shadows in the room around them. The dog groomed himself as he prepared for the night and the man lay back, dozing in and out of sleep.

"You are tired, good friend," said the dog, "and

it is late. Why do you not allow yourself to sleep?"

The man set aside the bottle of wine and looked at the dog. Then he rubbed his eyes and said, "If it were not for sleep I would be a happy man, for it is in dreams that my troubles torment me, and it is by dreams that I am homeless and most alone."

The dog thought about this and said, "It is not our dreams that make us, but we who make our dreams." Then he added, "Sleep well, fine man, and let not those things that are not yours to fear cause you discomfort. Sleep and in the morning we shall speak again."

The man and the dog bid each other good-night, and then the man, cradling his bottle of wine, fell into a deep slumber. The dog moved next to the man and lay facing him, keeping his gaze on his sleeping friend.

"I can tell you, gentle friend," spoke the dog quietly, "that you have never been homeless, nor are you alone. But you have yet to see that sleep and rest are not quite one and the same thing."

The man slept and finally the dog slept too. The man snored loudly but the dog did not mind. Sometimes the man would startle himself, waking himself from his sleep by the sound of his own snoring, but then he would sleep again. The dog saw this but did not leave the side of his friend.

In his sleep the man dreamed. He would be happy and then he would be sad. There were people with him in his dreams whom he loved and sometimes he would laugh out loud, whereas other times he would cry and the dog would be concerned.

"What is it that troubles you, dear friend?" said the dog, but the man was sleeping and the dog spoke the words without wanting to wake his friend.

The man dreamed about a woman. He was very happy when he was with her in the dream and there was a little girl who was with them also. There was great joy for him in the dream and the man smiled and giggled as he slept. But then something in the dream made him remember that the woman and the little girl were gone and so he wept though he did not wake.

This worried the dog but still he did not bother the man.

In another dream somebody was asking the man how old he was and so he blurted, "26!" But then he would say, "No – 56!" and would start laughing but the laughter died away and in the dream the man wondered where all the time had gone and so he would cry again.

By the time morning came both the man and the dog were sleeping deeply. The sun shone through a window at the far eastern side of the building and finally the light found its way to them. It was the dog who woke first.

"Ah," said the dog, "it is morning and the sun has come to find us. Have you slept well, good friend?"

The man was slow to open his eyes but then he sat upright and answered the dog.

"It has been a night like any other," said the man, "but yes, I have slept well, thank you."

"Good," said the dog, "the morning is here and the day is new."

The man looked at the dog and said the day was always the day. The dog answered yes, but this was a day that no one had seen before and so it was new and would be different from other days.

"Perhaps," said the man, but he was not sure he understood and so he said nothing more.

They shared the quiet of the morning as the sun found its way through the east window. They each took a drink of water and then ate some of the food that was left from the evening before. The man went to the faucet that leaked water and washed a little whereas the dog groomed himself.

The morning warmed and they agreed they would go out and walk. The man was used to spending his days seeking money and the dog understood this.

"It is admirable," said the dog, "that you seek the means to buy your needs and do not steal."

The man said he was not a thief but just a man. He had seen hard times and came close to stealing in the past but could not make himself go through with it.

"I am fortunate that in the end I have not had

to steal," said the man. "Something always seems to happen that I do not need to."

The dog looked at the man who was thin and had endured much suffering. He was happy for the man at that moment and said, "Yes, something always happens and you have much reason to be proud."

They walked down a long street, passing people who were on their way to work. There was great activity at this time of the morning as the city came alive, and the dog could tell that the man enjoyed this. The man would smile at people, though he did not know them, and would sometimes say hello and good morning.

"You enjoy this," said the dog.

"Yes," said the man, "it is good to watch the city come alive."

"Well," said the dog, "we, too, are a part of it."

They continued and the dog wanted to ask the man about the night and his dreams.

"You snore deeply," said the dog.

"Ah, that is true," said the man. "It reminds me that I am alive."

The dog understood this.

"And you have dreams," said the dog.

"Yes," responded the man. "I have dreams."

They walked further and the dog spoke again.

"You dream of those things that are closest to your heart," said the dog.

The man nodded.

"The lady and the little girl," said the dog. "They were very special to you."

Now the man stopped to look at the dog. He did not know how the dog knew of the lady or the little girl who were in his dreams, but he did not ask.

"Yes," said the man, "they were very special to me. The lady was beautiful and had the heart of an angel. She was my wife," spoke the man and then he was quiet.

They wound their way through some narrow streets where street lamps still shone. The dog was quiet and knew the man would talk again.

"It was long ago and I do not remember well," continued the man. "I hurt her or she hurt me, I do not remember. But what does this matter now? It was long ago and I do not know."

"You have not seen her?" asked the dog.

"No, I have not seen her," said the man. "But she is in my dreams and makes my heart heavy with sadness."

"Then you love her and know that she loves you," said the dog.

The man looked at the dog and wondered why a dog would say such a thing.

"And what of the little girl?" asked the dog.

"The little girl was my daughter," said the man, "and now she is dead."

The man stopped walking and it looked like he would fall over. His eyes grew full of water and soon he was crying. He sat on the curb and put his head down. He was very sad and the dog was sad for him.

"She is well," said the dog. "I promise you this, and I promise you also that she is very happy," added the dog.

But the man was crying and so the dog sat down beside him.

"How would you know this?" said the man. "You are only a dog."

"I know it as would any other," said the dog,

"be it man or dog."

But the man did not understand and so the dog was quiet. Finally, the man stopped crying and said, "You are a good dog."

The dog said, "Thank you," and asked if the man wanted to dry his face on the dog's fur. This made the man laugh and so the dog was glad also. They got up and the man decided they should keep going.

"That is always a wise decision," said the dog.

They passed a bakery where a woman came out and gave a cup of coffee and a small bag of donuts to the man.

"The coffee is hot and the donuts are fresh," said the woman. "I am sorry that I have nothing for your dog."

The man smiled and looked down at the dog. "That is okay, good lady," said the man. "He is a very special dog and prefers to dine only at the finest of establishments, where I happen to know he enjoys a good feast."

The woman looked surprised and then the man and the woman laughed together.

Later, after the man and the dog were on their way again, the dog said, "That was very clever of you. You flatter me. Yet," continued the dog, "there is great truth in humour."

A little gust of wind beat down the street and flew past them. The dog closed his eyes and lifted his head to feel the breeze and the man held his collar tight around his neck. The dog enjoyed the breath of wind while the man waited for it to pass. The dog remarked that it was a warm wind and felt like a gentle caress whereas the man said the wind was just the wind.

"But surely you feel more than just moving

air," said the dog. "It was not meant to disturb us or make us uncomfortable," continued the dog.

"Then what is the wind?" asked the man.

"A gentle breath," exclaimed the dog, "and a reminder of all that lives and breathes, for all creation is alive."

The man looked at the dog, who had become very animated. The dog's eyes were wide and bright and the man thought now he could see a smile on the face of the dog. Another gentle wind blew past them and again the dog closed his eyes and faced into the wind.

"Ah," said the dog, "again – like a loving hand moving over us."

But again the man felt only the wind. The dog was happy but he could see that the man was puzzled.

"Let us go to the park," said the dog.

They turned west and headed toward a little area of park where there were flowers and trees and grass. There was a pond in the middle of the park and they found a quiet bench where they could sit and rest. People and animals were in the park and it was very peaceful.

"And what do we do now?" asked the man.

"Let us just sit," said the dog and so he sat on the bench next to the man.

The trees and the grass were very green because it was still August and all the flowers were in bloom and were very beautiful. They watched a small child play in a foot pond where he tried to sail a small toy boat that kept wanting to capsize. People walked through the park. Some were with friends and some were alone, and some even had their own dogs with them. Everyone was unhurried and the sounds of the city faded into the background.

The man and the dog sat and said nothing for a long time and then the dog asked, "What do you see?"

The man thought about this and blurted, "Dogs and trees!" and then started to laugh.

They sat some more and a little boy ran past them trying to get a kite into the air. The kite was bright orange and yellow and the dog's eyes opened wide as the kite caught the tip of a zephyr and took flight.

"Wonderful!" exclaimed the dog. "Do you see? Where moments ago there was nothing now there is a child who has found the wind and taken flight in it!"

The man smiled and looked on. He had been to the park before and had seen the children play.

"Yes, it is good," said the man. But when the dog looked at him the dog did not think the man saw anything but a boy and a kite.

"Look at the trees," said the dog.

"Yes," said the man. "I see the trees."

"What do you see?"

"Trees!" said the man.

"Look closely," said the dog. "Watch the leaves."

A gentle wind, like the one they had felt before and given rise to the boy's kite, washed over the trees. All the leaves danced with the gentle rhythm of the wind and the dog was pleased.

"Do you see?" asked the dog. "Do you hear? There is great joy among them. They dance and sing with the wind!"

The man looked at the dog and shook his head.

"You are only a dog," said the man. "What do you know of 'dancing and singing leaves?' – there is only the wind and the trees. But yes, it is very nice."

The dog was silent and decided to watch and listen to the magic that surrounded them. He listened to the beautiful song in the park that was shared by the trees and flowers and even the water in the pond. Many of the people and the animals were part of the wonderful chorus even though there were those who did not know this. When he looked at the man, the man was just sitting there with a simple smile on his face and so the dog said nothing for a long time.

Finally the dog said, "We can leave now."

The man said he was ready and so they got up to leave the park. The dog was very happy and said this had been good for him.

"There are more things to feast upon than food," said the dog.

But the man did not respond and the dog could see that he truly did not understand. Yet the dog was happy for himself because he knew that the gifts he had taken pleasure in were there for all those to enjoy who chose to see them.

They went back into the heart of the city and the man begged a little money from the people whom they passed. The dog stood by and watched as the man sometimes took a dollar and other times got a penny. Other people passed and gave nothing.

The man remarked at one point that, "not everyone gives," and the dog responded that giving and receiving were often one and the same thing and that one must plant in the garden in order to take from the garden.

"What, do you speak now of 'garden'?" asked the man. "It is only money I require so that we may have some food and so I will again buy myself some wine."

"Yes," said the dog. "Wine is good because it is

the fruit of the earth – another piece of the world that gives of itself."

The man now grew upset with the dog.

"You are a very strange dog," said the man. "You speak of leaves and gardens and wine and yet you are only a dog. And," continued the man, "you say you will not take wine because it is that you *are* a dog."

"The gifts we receive need not be ours alone," answered the dog. "I am glad that you enjoy wine and know that you take some comfort in it. Still," said the dog, "it is true that I am only a dog."

The man decided there was good reason why a dog was only a dog and went back to asking for money. The dog stood by quietly and the two were silent for a long time.

It was late in the day when the man decided he had enough money and so the two went on their way to a place where the man knew he could get food cheaply. The pair went down a series of long winding streets. The sun had dropped low in the west and the air was cooler. There was a bit of chill but the man did not seem bothered by this and the dog had his own coat of fur to keep him warm.

"Soon the colours of fall will be upon us and it will be cooler," said the dog. "It would be wise if we knew a place that would keep us warm for the cold months ahead."

"Yes," said the man, "the cold months will come, but now I wish to have some wine and food."

On the way to the market they passed a little wine shop where the man had been before. He said to the dog that if the dog didn't mind, he would just go in to take a look, "for later," said the man.

"As you wish," said the dog.

When the man came out, he had a brown paper bag and the dog knew he had bought some wine. The man said they should go and so they continued to walk. After walking for a while, the man turned to the dog and said, "There is something I must tell you."

The dog said okay and the man confessed that he spent what money they had on the wine and would not now be able to buy their food.

"I am very sorry," said the man. "I did not mean this to be so. I wanted only to see the wine I would have later and now there will be no food tonight."

The dog could tell the man was very sorry and said, "Do not concern yourself, good friend. It is not your place to feed me. But I would say you need to watch that you have control over the wine and that the wine does not have control over you."

The dog knew he would be hungry tonight and

yet he did not judge the man for what he had done.

"I hope you will enjoy your wine tonight," said the dog, "and that the wine is worthy of such a fine man."

The man looked at the dog and felt very bad. He said that perhaps they could beg some more but it was getting late and soon it would be dark. The man tried to stop the occasional stranger and get more money but people hurried on, not wanting to stop to help a man and a dog in the street.

It was now dark and they were not successful. It was agreed between them that they would go to the old building where they had spent the night before.

"It gave us shelter from the night and was a good place to lay our heads," said the dog. And so they went on their way.

When they arrived at the old building they

made themselves comfortable with the old blankets and again the man lit some candles. The dog was happy to see the light and remarked that the light of one candle could diffuse all the surrounding dark.

"Yet all darkness cannot smother a single little flame," commented the dog.

The man opened his bottle of wine and the dog had the bone from the evening before. The dog was happy to have the bone and remarked that it was a very good bone but knew too that there was no food for the man.

"Even though I would not have your wine," said the dog, "I would share my bone with you."

The man looked at the dog and laughed.

"That is okay, dog," said the man, "I will not share your bone." And then he laughed again.

The hour grew late and soon the man was dozing from the effects of the wine. Then he was falling asleep and snoring loudly. The dog put aside his bone and went to lay next to the man as he did the night before.

"Sleep well, good man," said the dog, "and listen to the sounds that say you live."

The man slept deeply and soon he was dreaming. He dreamed again of the beautiful woman and then again of the little girl. He thought he would be very sad in the dream but this time he was happy. The man and the woman were together in the dream and together they were happy. Then the little girl was talking to him and asked him to come with her. He saw the dog in the dream and the dog was telling him something important that made him very glad but he could not remember what it was. He knew only that he was very happy to be with the woman and the girl and the dog was happy also.

At one point in the night his snoring made him wake from his dream and when he opened his eyes the dog was there watching him.

"Ah," said the man, "you see? Again my snoring wakes me. But it is good to know I am alive. I was making dreams," said the man and then he laughed.

"Yes," said the dog, "it is true that we can make a dream but it is also true that a dream can make us."

The man closed his eyes and the dog said he should sleep again. The man said the dog was a good dog and then he was asleep.

By the time morning came the man had slept well and the dog had not left his side. When the man got up he wanted to tell the dog something about his dream but he could not remember what it was.

"I only know that it was a good dream," said the man. "It gave me a glad heart but I do not know why. I must be a very silly man."

The dog told the man that it was okay not to remember a dream and that dreams were like banquets. "Sometimes we do not remember a great meal but that does not mean it has not done us well," said the dog.

The man looked at the dog and thought he remembered something important about the dog in his dream but then he forgot and did not speak of it again.

When the man and the dog went out that morning the man walked slower than usual and the dog was concerned.

"Do not worry," said the man. "It is just that I need a bit of food, for last night we did not eat."

"Perhaps," said the dog, "it would be wise to go to the shelter and see if they will help us."

The man thought this was a good idea and so they went to the shelter that helped homeless men. The dog had not been to the shelter with the man before and so the dog spoke of what he saw.

"There are many," said the dog.

"Yes," said the man, "there are many – and I am one of the many."

"Not quite," said the dog, "there are different stories here, and equally," continued the dog, "lives of different choices."

The man wondered about this and responded, "Well then, dog," he said, "what choice is it that leads a man to such a point in his life as this? And, who is it who would select such a fate?"

The dog answered that, yes, life was a curious thing full of learning and experience, and that such answers were not always revealed in the lives of those who lived.

The man thought about this. "You speak in riddles, dog," retorted the man. "So where is it then that a man finds these answers?" asked the man.

"Faith," answered the dog.

They continued past many men in the shelter. Some were very downtrodden and some were very sick. Others looked quite sad and there were those who only slept.

They came to one old man who had a bright sparkle in his eyes. When the old man saw the dog he looked up and said, "Ah – a dog! I have not spoken to a dog for a long time."

"Be careful with this dog," said the man, "he is very clever and will outsmart you if he wishes, though I have noticed that that is not what he wishes." Then the man winked at the old man.

But the old man just petted the dog and the dog did not mind. He was happy that the old man was happy.

Later, when the man and the dog continued, the dog said, "Sometimes it is the simplest pleasures that give us the greatest joy."

They went to the back of the shelter where there was a kitchen. People there were very busy. They were running around and working so that they could serve others in the shelter. There, the man asked for some food and water for himself and the dog.

The man and the dog stood waiting while someone went to get them food and water and the dog watched very closely.

"This is very good," said the dog. "Do you see? Do you see the way of things?"

The man was watching also but did not understand the dog.

"What do you mean?" said the man. "I have been here many times and I see what I have always seen before."

"And what is that?" asked the dog.

"People working," said the man.

"But what is it they do?" persisted the dog.

The man looked at the dog and frowned. To the man it was all very obvious.

"People clean and make coffee and get food," said the man. He shook his head at the dog. He thought the dog was very odd.

"This is not a place where one grows rich," explained the dog, "they come here to give service."

The dog stood admiring all who participated in making the shelter a haven and place of refuge. It was a sanctuary for the weak, the infirm, the brokenhearted, the downtrodden, and the lost.

"All here give of themselves," said the dog. "It is selfless work they do. *That* is the way of things."

But the man had not thought this before and said, "I am sure they get paid."

"Yes," replied the dog, "they are compensated – but not in the way you think."

A young lady came and gave them food and water. She was young and had a very gentle manner about her. After she left, the dog said, "She reminds you of your daughter. She was kind also," continued the dog.

But the man did not know how the dog knew of such things. He was quiet as they ate and drank.

When they were done, they agreed they would go and so they got up to leave the shelter. When they got to the door, the man turned to look at the homeless people there and those helping them. He watched for a while and then he turned to the dog.

"Not everyone wishes to help themselves," said the man. "That is what I see."

"That is true," said the dog. "Yet those helping know they must not give up on the others."

They ventured outdoors and it was now an overcast day with clouds that had come in from the north. Both the man and the dog felt a chill and decided they would return to the building where they had spent the night before.

"We should stay indoors today," said the man. Yet after walking for a while, the dog turned and said, "It is curious. We were already indoors where food and shelter were available and companionship was offered. Yet you will not return there. Why is that?" asked the dog.

The man stopped. "It is not as you think," said the man. "I have stayed there before."

"Then why do we not return?" said the dog.

"Because in that place," said the man, "I do not like what I see."

This time the dog said nothing but instead continued on his way and now the man followed.

When they arrived at the building they both stopped. There were many men there with big machines and cranes and they were tearing the old building down. It was very busy and the sounds were very loud. The man and the dog watched and listened to the sound of brick and stone crumble to the ground as the men worked.

"It is as with many things," said the dog.

The dog looked overhead to see that the clouds were growing dark and then he looked back at the old building that was being destroyed.

"A decision is being made for us," said the dog. "If we wish to go indoors we must return to the shelter where we were this morning."

The man was not happy with this idea but there was nothing else to do and so he agreed as well that they should return to the shelter.

But when they got back to the shelter it was very busy and there was no place for them.

"Others seek shelter as well," said the dog, "and now it is too late and there is no room for us."

The man and the dog thought about this and decided they would go back to the park.

"But first," suggested the dog, "let us see if we can get a little food to take with us for later."

They went back to the kitchen but this time it was very crowded and, when they approached, the same young woman who had served them before was there again.

"I am very sorry," said the young woman, "but there are many mouths to feed and now we have run out." She looked very sad and the dog knew she wanted to help but that she did not know what to do. She went away and when she came back she brought a big bone and said to the man, "All I have is this soup bone for your dog. I am sure he will like it very much but there is nothing for you and now the kitchen is bare."

The man looked troubled but he thanked the young lady for the bone and assured her that, yes, the dog would like it very much and had in the past offered to share his bones with the man.

"That is very funny," said the young woman, "but then you must be a kind man and he must be a very good dog."

"Oh, yes," said the man, "he is quite the dog."

When she went away again the dog said, "You must not worry. You said yourself that things always seemed to work out. Let us find a place to sit and we will wait."

The man and the dog found a corner where they sat together and waited. An hour later there were some very excited voices coming from the kitchen and then a man with a big booming voice called out with some good news.

"I have some good news," said the man with the big booming voice. "Meat and bread are being delivered and everyone will have food again.

"You see," said the dog, "again we are shown that we will not be abandoned."

The man and the dog waited with the many

others and then they received their food.

"Take it and enjoy," said the young lady in the kitchen to the man. "I have given you a bit extra for your dog as well." Then she smiled and the man smiled also.

"And now again we will eat and we will be well again," said the dog.

"But where will we go?" asked the man, "there is no room for us here."

"We will return to the park," answered the dog. "Nature will welcome us."

As they continued, the dog noticed that the man still moved slowly.

"Just a little further, good man," said the dog, "soon you will be able to eat and take rest."

The sky was now dark and the wind began to blow. As they entered the park it began to rain and the dog knew that the man would be cold.

"Let us find a big tree with a bench," said the dog, "where we will be protected and entertained by the coming storm."

They found just such a tree as the thunder struck and the rain began. The dog made the man take the food and begin to eat.

"I am sorry that we do not have wine for you today," said the dog.

"That is okay, dog," said the man, "today is a good day without the wine."

Soon the storm was raging. The wind howled and the rain fell but the big tree above them protected them as they ate. When they were finished, the dog told the man that he should rest and the dog would protect him while he slept.

"I will stay next to you so that you will keep

warm," said the dog, "and I will be here to protect you so you will be safe also," and soon the man was asleep.

The dog watched closely as the man closed his eyes and fell into a deep slumber. The dog lay very close to the man to keep him warm and the dog enjoyed the warmth of the man also.

The storm raged on but the man was not bothered for he slept deeply. Soon he was snoring and the sound of his snoring kept rhythm with the thunder of the storm and the breathing of the dog.

The dog observed this and commented, "Yes, it is true that we are all one." Then, the dog allowed himself to put his head down and rest.

In his sleep, the man returned to a dream where he was with the dog and the dog was showing him many wonderful things. There were people and places in the dream that the man had long ago forgotten and in the dream the beautiful woman and the little girl returned.

He saw himself as a young man and then as a little boy, and then he was the man again and it was like a big picture show where everything was made clear and there were no questions.

He snored deeply and at one point late into the evening, the man woke and was laughing and he said to the dog, "I was listening to the wind! – and the trees! – and the leaves! They make joy! And laughter! And music!" and then he laughed again and said, "but you are just a dog, how would you know such things?" and then again he laughed and went back to sleep.

Late into the night, when the storm had quieted down and was very calm, the man woke and said, "You have been a very good dog, and I humbly give thanks to you, good friend." Then he petted the dog and returned to sleep.

There was music from the wind and the trees for the man and in the music he heard the voice of his little girl.

"She calls to me," he said.

Then he made a comment that surprised even the dog.

"Our sleeping and our waking are one in the same, aren't they?" said the man.

"They are shadows of one another," said the dog and then they both were quiet.

It was in the early hours of morning, before the sun rose and the night air was still and peaceful, that the man stopped snoring. The dog lifted his head and nudged the man, but the man made no sound and did not move. Nor did he snore.

The dog waited as the sun rose and, gradually, the city came alive and people entered the park, but the dog did not leave the man's side.

By the time the day was underway, when the sun shone bright and the park was busy, someone noticed the dog on the bench beside the man.

"Does your master sleep, boy?" they asked. But then they could see the man was not asleep and so they said, "Wait here, boy," and went to get help.

By the time the ambulance arrived, the dog had still not left the man. Two young attendants checked the man on the bench and then one shook his head and said, "Sorry, boy."

But the dog did not say anything because he was only a dog.

There were many people gathered around and the dog waited as they carried the man away. Then, when the ambulance drove off, the dog slipped through the people and continued on his way, unnoticed.

There was a peaceful little breeze and now the sun cast beautiful platinum rays of light down on the park surrounding everyone. The dog walked through the park and when he was at a safe distance, he turned to look at the people and the ambulance with the man and whispered, "Have a good journey, my friend."

Then, the dog lifted his head and, closing his eyes, turned into the wind.

Also by Duane Hewitt:

A Hard Way To Die
Three Novellas
ISBN 0-9682522-8-1

To contact the author, please call or write:

P.O. Box 455
31 Adelaide Street East
Toronto, Ontario
Canada
M5C 2J5
Toll Free: 1-888-272-2152